On ANZAC Day

Dawn McMillan

At school, my teacher told us about ANZAC Day.
ANZAC Day is a special day.

At home, I sent an email to Grandpa.
I told him about ANZAC Day.

Dear Grandpa,
ANZAC Day is on 25 April.
On ANZAC Day, we think about people who went to war.

We think about soldiers.
The soldiers went to war.

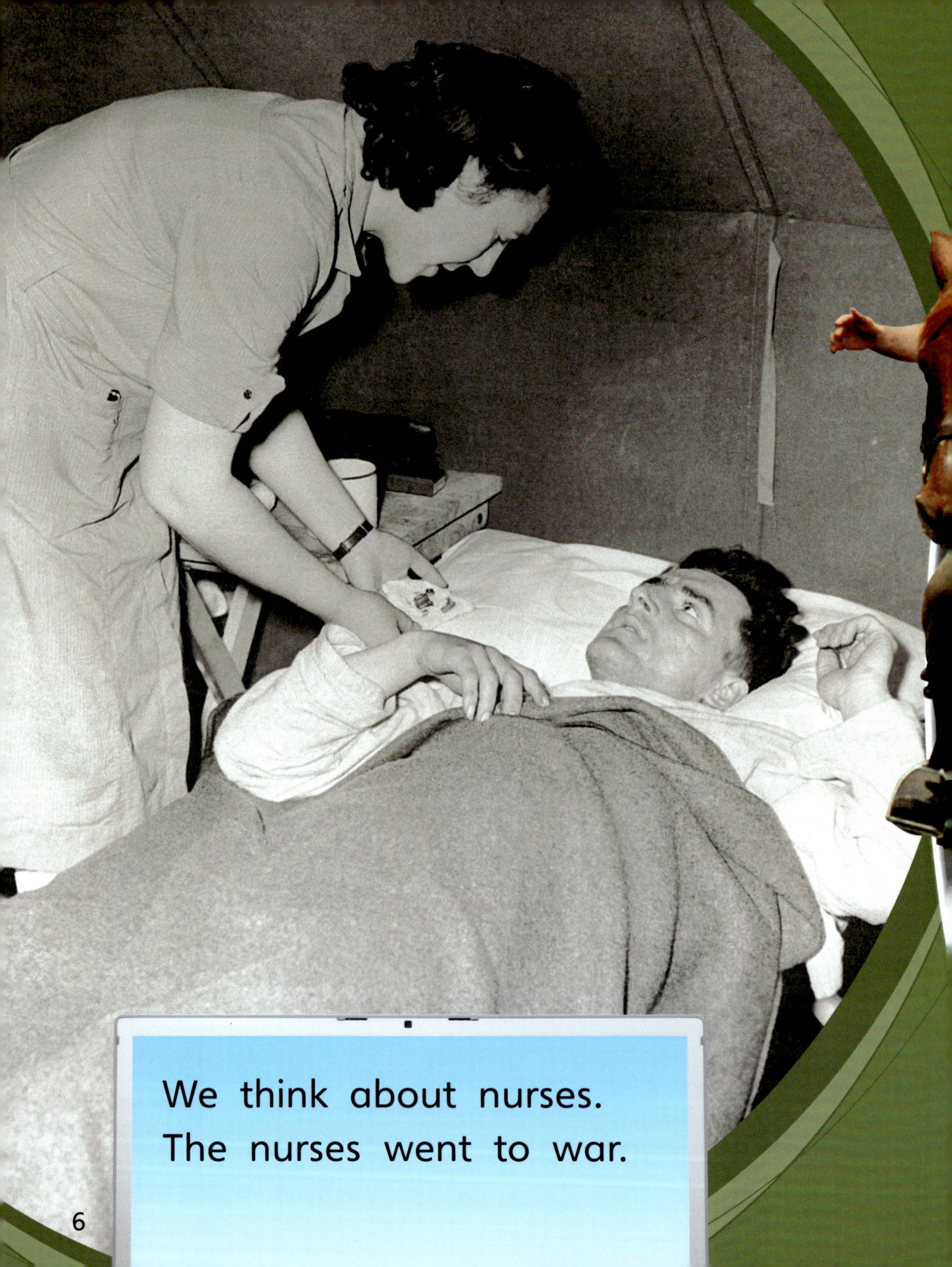

We think about nurses.
The nurses went to war.

Lots of people have been to war.

They went to war to keep
us safe.

On ANZAC Day, we will stay quiet for a short time.
We will think about the people who went to war.

We will thank them
at the ANZAC Day parade.

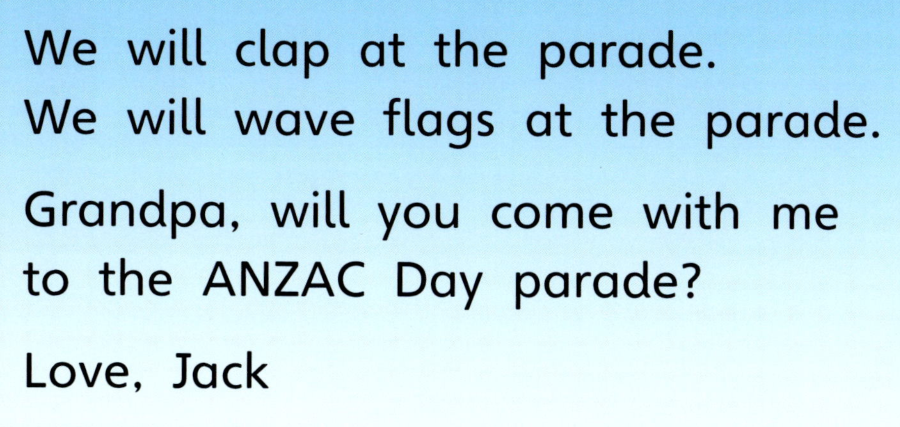

We will clap at the parade.
We will wave flags at the parade.

Grandpa, will you come with me to the ANZAC Day parade?

Love, Jack

Dear Jack,
I will come with you
to the ANZAC Day parade.

My grandpa was a soldier. He went to war long ago. He went on a boat.

Jack, I will wear a poppy on ANZAC Day.
You can wear my grandpa's medals.

We will wave and clap.
We will thank the people
who went to war
to keep us safe.

Love, Grandpa

Dear Grandpa,
Thank you for coming
to ANZAC Day with me.

I would like to go every year
to say thank you.

Love,
Jack